# Orca's Family
## and More Northwest Coast Stories

Learning From Nature and the World Around Us

Stories and Illustrations

## Robert James Challenger

First Edition 1997, second printing 2002, third printing 2004, fourth printing 2012

HERITAGE HOUSE PUBLISHING COMPANY LTD.
heritagehouse.ca


Library and Archives Canada Cataloguing in Publication

Challenger, Robert James, 1953-
   Orca's family and more Northwest Coast stories

   ISBN 978-1-895811-39-1

   1. Nature stories, Canadian (English)*  2. Children's stories, Canadian (English)*  I. Title

PS8555.H277072 1997      jC813'.54      C97-910625-7      PZ7.C34980r 1997


All Illustrations: Robert James Challenger
Book design and layout: Darlene Nickull
Edited by:  Rhonda Bailey

Heritage House acknowledges the financial support for its publishing program from the Government of Canada through the Canada Book Fund (CBF), Canada Council for the Arts and the province of British Columbia through the British Columbia Arts Council and the Book Publishing Tax Credit.

 Canadian Heritage  Patrimoine canadien       Canada Council for the Arts  Conseil des Arts du Canada       BRITISH COLUMBIA ARTS COUNCIL  Supported by the Province of British Columbia

Printed in Canada

# Dedication

Dedicated to my wife, Joannie,
and daughters, Kristi and Kari,
who taught me that
love is what life is for.

## Other books by Robert James Challenger

**Eagle's Reflection**
and Other Northwest Coast Stories
ISBN 978-1-895811-07-0

**Grizzly's Home**
and Other Northwest Coast Children's Stories
ISBN 978-1-894384-94-0

**Nature's Circle**
and Other Northwest Coast Children's Stories
ISBN 978-1-894384-77-3

**Raven's Call**
and More Northwest Coast Stories
ISBN 978-1-895811-91-9

**Salmon's Journey**
and More Northwest Coast Stories
ISBN 978-1-894384-34-6

All $9.95

*Wonderful Northwest Coast stories for kids … Jim Challenger is a real artist as his book demonstrates.*

—Ron MacIssac, Shaw Cable's "What's Happening?"

*I really loved your stories that you read to us. I really got the feeling of what you meant in your magical writing. Thank you for coming to our school to make us feel joyful. I enjoyed your stories!! Sincerely,*

—Josey L. (Age 8)

*Modern day fables are the right length. … knows how to write for the oral storyteller; the written words slip easily off the tongue.*

—*Times Colonist*

*Challenger's prose bears a deliberate resemblance to First Nations oral traditions: humans and nature interact freely, and both are capable of folly, repentance, and wisdom. In his artwork, Challenger also embraces West Coast Aboriginal culture by portraying his characters in exquisite Haida-style prints. Highly recommended.*

—Steve Pitt, *Canadian Book Review Annual*

# Contents

*Dedication*   3

*Orca's Family*   6

*Woodpecker's Friend*   8

*Cougar's Fear*   10

*How Beaver Built His Dam*   12

*Dolphin Shows the Way*   14

*Why Swallows Dance*   16

*Raccoon's Shame*   18

*Owl's Eyes and Ears*   20

*Crow's Call*   22

*Swan's Beautiful Feathers*   24

*Rainbow Trout's Colours*   26

*Elk's Antlers*   29

*Wild Horse*   32

*Grey Whale's Wish*   34

*Rockfish Finds a Home*   36

*Deer's Lesson*   38

*Rabbit's Great Escape*   40

*Fox's Flame*   42

*Raven and the Two-Headed Salmon*   45

# Orca's Family

The summer sunlight sparkled off the ripples on the ocean. Grandfather, Grandmother, and their two grandchildren sat in a fishing boat, slowly trolling along the shoreline.

Suddenly, as they looked out to sea, the water parted around the tip of a jet-black fin. Higher it rose until Orca's head broke the surface. Whoosh! came the sound as he exhaled, took a breath, and slipped beneath the water again. Behind him, two smaller curved dorsal fins revealed a female and a small calf keeping pace with Orca.

Grandmother said, "I see Orca and his mate are still together, and they have a little one with them this year."

One of the children asked, "Why do we never see just one Orca?"

Grandmother said, "When I was a little girl I was once out fishing with Raven and we saw Orca by himself. Orca looked very sad.

"Raven asked him, 'What is wrong?'

"Orca replied, 'I am lonely and hungry. When the sun goes down you get to go home. I must stay out here in the middle of the cold, deep ocean all by myself, and today I have not been able to catch any fish to eat.'

"I said, 'We have caught lots of fish,' and I gave him our biggest salmon.

"Raven said to Orca, 'Where is your family?'

"'I left my family when I was old enough to hunt on my own,' Orca replied. 'Without them around, all the fish I catch I get to keep for myself. I never have to share with the others.'

"Raven said, 'Well, that is true. Being part of a family does mean you have to share with others. But it also means that when you are hungry, they can share their fish with you, and when you are lonely, they are there to give you comfort.'

"The next time Raven and I saw Orca, he had a new mate with him. They swam over to where we were fishing.

"Orca said 'Thank you for telling me about the value of family. Now I have a mate and we swim together and share everything we catch. She is always there to take care of me and I am there to take care of her.'"

# Woodpecker's Friend

**M**an felt angry as he stomped down the path through the woods. He wished he could be out fishing instead of collecting firewood and food for the winter. The chores were taking a long time because there was no one to help him. He had called out to others for help, but they had not replied.

In fact, the other people had helped him many times in the past. One had helped Man cut the trees for his house. Another had brought him food when he was sick. And many others had made themselves available whenever he needed help.

Just above Man's head, a loud, "knock, knock, knock," rang out. He looked up to see the red head of Woodpecker pounding on the side of a big tree. "Knock, knock, knock," sounded out again.

Man asked, "Why are you knocking?"

Woodpecker replied, "When I need some food I call on my friends, the trees, and they let me eat the little insects that live in their bark. I have food, and the trees are happy because the insects aren't bothering them."

Man said, "I wish other people would help me like that. When I knock at their doors they do not answer. I knock louder and louder, but they will not come to help me with my chores."

Woodpecker asked, "What do you do when people come to you for help?"

"I don't have time to help them," Man snapped back. "I have work to do, and when I have some time I want to have fun, not go and do other people's work."

Woodpecker said to him, "True friends always give more than they receive."

Man thought about that and replied, "You are right. I will try to help other people more. Perhaps then I will make friends who will be there for me when I really need them."

# Cougar's Fear

The flicker of campfire light illuminated Grandfather's weathered face as he sat in the forest with his young grandson.

The boy looked up and said, "I'm not afraid to camp out when you are here, Grandfather."

"We all have fears," said the old man. "Even I am sometimes afraid, but I do not let my fear defeat me."

"What would happen if you did let it defeat you?" asked his grandson.

Grandfather threw more wood on the fire and said, "Many years ago, there was a little boy who was afraid of everything.

"One morning, Eagle was flying overhead and heard an awful racket below. The boy was crying so loud that he had woken all the birds and animals. They all started chirping, calling, roaring, and barking.

"Eagle landed beside the boy and asked, 'Why are you making such a sad sound? You are scaring everyone around you.'

"The boy answered, 'I want to go and play with the other children in the forest, but I am afraid I will get lost and never find my way back.' He continued to wail.

"Eagle said, 'The forest is a big place, but if you stay with your friends you will be safe.'

"The boy said, 'But what if I am attacked by a wild animal?' and he continued to cry even louder.

"Eagle could not stand the sound of the boy's screeching. 'Well, I know one way to make sure you aren't attacked by a wild animal,' Eagle said, and transformed the boy into Cougar.

"Eagle said to Cougar, 'You will never succeed at anything if your fear keeps you from trying. Go out and start to learn to take chances. Otherwise you will have to live your life in the shadows instead of running in the sun.'

"But Cougar never did learn. He just crept into the deep forest, where even today we still hear his fearful cries."

# How Beaver Built His Dam

The morning sun spread its warm light onto the forest on the far side of the lake. Grandfather and his grandson fished from their canoe as it slowly drifted in the early morning mist.

Near the end of the lake, Beaver left a trail of ripples on the calm water as he towed a branch towards his dam.

The child whispered to Grandfather, "How did such a little animal build such a big dam?"

"Well," Grandfather replied, "Many years ago, Beaver only had a little pond.

"One day Raven overheard Beaver complaining.

"Raven asked, 'What is the problem?'

"Beaver replied, 'Every year the summer sun dries up my pond and leaves me with no place to swim.'

"Raven suggested, 'If you built a dam, it would make your pond deeper and keep it from drying up each year.'

"Beaver looked at Raven. 'Are you crazy? How am I going to build a dam big enough to hold that much water? I cannot fall a tree big enough to block the stream.'

"'You are right. You are too small to bring down such a large tree. But you are big enough to fall a lot of little trees,' said Raven.

"'That would take forever,' said Beaver. 'I don't have time.'

"Raven laughed at him. 'If you had used the time you have spent complaining, your dam would have been built long ago.'

"So Beaver got started. Raven watched him as he slowly added one branch at a time. By the next year, Beaver had a dam built right across the stream and his pond had water in it all summer long.

"Beaver said, 'Thank you, Raven. You were right, I could build a big dam—one stick at a time.'

"Raven smiled and said to Beaver, 'I knew you could if you tried.'"

# Dolphin Shows the Way

**G**randfather and his grandson were taking wood to their neighbour's house. The neighbour was caring for his sick wife and not able to get the wood himself.

The grandson asked, "How much do you think they will pay us for bringing in their wood?"

Grandfather said, "Perhaps we will be repaid in a way you don't expect."

His grandson looked puzzled. "What do you mean?" he asked.

Grandfather replied with a story. "Many years ago there was a woman who was very wise. Whenever someone was in need she would help them. She never asked for anything in return.

"One day she became deathly ill. Her friends were very worried.

"Soaring overhead, Eagle saw the people's concern and offered to help. Eagle took the woman down to the ocean and transformed her into a sleek, healthy Dolphin.

"Many years later Dolphin came across a boat drifting far out at sea.

"In it was a man, who cried out, 'Help me. I cannot find my way home.'

"Dolphin said to him, 'Follow me and I will lead you home.'

"Dolphin swam ahead of the man's boat, and in a few hours he was back in the bay in front of his house.

"He said to Dolphin, 'How can I repay you?'

"Dolphin replied, 'Eagle once helped me and I am just glad that I could help show you the way,' and she swam away.

"Later that year, the man was out in the forest and found Eagle lying on the ground with a broken wing.

"He said to Eagle, 'Let me fix your wing.'

"Eagle said, 'But I have nothing to pay you with.'

"The man replied, 'You do not need to. You already paid me when you helped Dolphin. Dolphin in turn helped me by showing me the way home. Now it is only right that I can help you.'"

Grandfather looked at his grandson and said, "Always be like Dolphin. When you see someone who has lost their way, help them find their path again. Do not ask for anything in return, for someday you may be the lost one, and you will be glad there are kind souls like Dolphin to help guide you in the right direction."

# Why Swallows Dance

Grandmother and Grandfather sat on the beach watching the sun set, as they had for fifty years. High above, in the dim light, two small birds with long, flowing tails fluttered through the air. The couple watched them, then turned to each other and smiled.

"After all these years," Grandfather said, "your slippers are still dancing."

Grandmother laughed. "Yes, they still are young and full of energy like I was when I was a little girl."

Her granddaughter overheard them and asked Grandmother, "Why did Grandfather call those birds your dancing slippers?"

Grandmother replied, "Come sit with Grandfather and me, and I will tell you the Swallows' story."

"Many years ago when I was a little girl like you, I loved to dance. For my birthday my mother bought me a special pair of dancing slippers. They were blue with gold trim, and had long laces that tied up around my legs.

"I wore those slippers all the time. I practised every day and eventually I became a dancer. I danced for myself and for other people.

"One day while I was dancing, I tripped and twisted my knee. At first, I thought it would heal, but after months it became clear that I would never dance again.

"I was sad and angry. All those years of practice were lost.

"I opened my window and threw my beautiful dancing slippers out into the cold rain. As I watched them fall, they started to change. The slippers grew wings and their long laces became the trailing tail feathers of two graceful blue and gold swallows.

"I watched the birds and realized that although my days of dancing were over, the joy I had felt and given to others would live on as long as swallows fly in the evening air."

Grandmother hugged her granddaughter and said, "You are young, so take advantage of the energy of youth to do whatever you desire. As you grow older and your body no longer lets you continue, do not be bitter. The joy goes on, just like the Swallows' dance."

# Raccoon's Shame

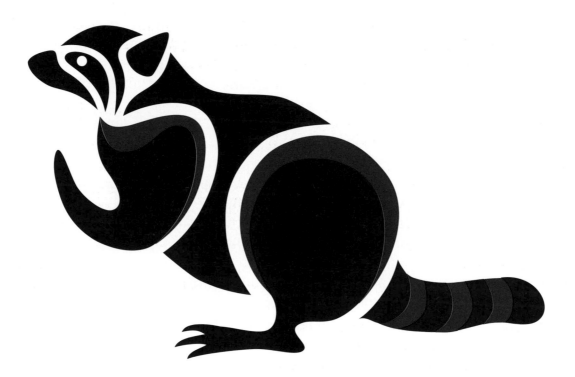

It was early dawn and the sun's first bright rays were just touching the treetops above the beach. A girl watched Raccoon wander along the mud flats and the shallow water. Using his nimble claws, he dug up crayfish and crabs. Before eating, Raccoon always washed each piece over and over again in the ocean water.

The girl asked Raccoon, "Why do you wash every piece of food before you eat it?"

Raccoon replied, "Many years ago I was an old man who lived near here.

"One day I complained to my neighbour, 'You are lucky. You always have enough food from your garden to last you through the winter. My garden is full of weeds and my plants hardly grow.'

"My neighbour replied, 'To have a good garden you have to work hard.'

"I told him, 'I know an easier way.'

"That night I put on a robber's mask, crept into his garden, and took all the food he had grown.

"As I returned to my house with the stolen food, I found Raven waiting for me.

"Raven said to me, 'Those are very nice vegetables you have there. Would you mind telling me where you bought them so I can buy some too?'

"I could not very well tell him that I had stolen them, so I didn't answer.

"Raven looked at me and said, 'Why, just this morning I saw your neighbour and his wife working in their garden. They were growing vegetables just like those you have here.'

"I confessed what I had done.

"Raven said to me, 'It is wrong to steal.'

"That is when Raven transformed me into Raccoon, with my robber's mask still covering my eyes and a ring on my tail for every piece of food I had stolen.

"Now, I wash everything I eat. I am forever trying to wash off the shame of taking something that did not belong to me."

# Owl's Eyes and Ears

The moon's light shone through the trees surrounding a small home in the forest. A girl and her little brother sat on the front porch stairs. She was reading a book and explaining the words and pictures to him.

Through the still air, Owl called from the forest, "Whooo?"

The girl replied, "It is me, and my brother."

The girl searched for the bird, but could not see it. She called softly, "Owl, where are you?"

In a nearby tree Owl turned her head and the light of the moon reflected from her eyes like two lights. Owl said, "I am up here. I was listening to you teach your brother about the stories in the book."

"Why, Owl?" asked the girl.

"I thought I might learn something new," came the reply.

"Owl, you are already so smart. What could you possibly learn from me?"

Owl glided down out of the tree and landed on the porch rail beside the little girl and boy.

Owl looked at them and said, "I have two eyes, just like you. I use my eyes to observe the colours of nature, the creatures of our world, and the clouds in the sky. Every day I learn something new from watching everything around me.

"I also have two ears, just like you. I use my ears to listen to the stories that others have to tell. From their stories I also learn something new every day."

The girl asked, "So if you have learned so much, why don't you talk more? You must have lots of things to say by now."

Owl replied, "When animals like you, your brother, and I were created, we were given two eyes to see the world and two ears to listen to its sounds. However, we were only given one mouth to talk with. I think that means we are supposed to watch and listen twice as much as we are meant to talk.

"Remember that you do not learn by talking. You learn by watching and listening to the world around you. Once you have learned, then you are ready to talk about it to others who are willing to listen and learn from you."

# Crow's Call

**R**aven sat in a tall tree, listening to the laughter of children playing in the meadow below. He loved to watch them tumble head-over-heels down the grassy hillside or run like the wind with their arms stretched out like Eagle's wings.

A group of three boys caught Raven's attention. These boys acted differently from the other children. When they were playing, they would shout at the others and tease them until they cried.

Then the boys would laugh, "Haw, haw, haw."

Raven called to them, "Please stop making the other children sad."

One of the boys replied, "We can do whatever we want. We are bigger and stronger than they are."

Raven watched as the boys took the other children's toys and broke them on the ground. Soon all the other children were crying.

The boys just laughed at them, "Haw, haw, haw."

The happy sounds of the other children faded as the group of three boys stole their fun.

Well, it didn't take long for Raven to get tired of watching that. He swooped down and picked up the boys by their collars and dumped them into the black mud by the stream. They stood up, covered in dirt from head to foot. Then, Raven transformed them into a circle of small black Crows, and chased them out of the meadow and over to the other side of the forest.

Now, Crows have to live far away. If they come too close, Raven chases them off because nobody wants to listen to the "haw, haw, haw" of their cruel laughter.

# Swan's Beautiful Feathers

Grandmother was out walking, enjoying the cool fall weather. She was not looking forward to the dark days of winter, so was taking advantage of every moment to savour the last of the nice weather.

As she came around the bend in the path, she saw her youngest granddaughter sitting on a big stone with tears streaming down her face.

Grandmother hurried over and asked, "What is wrong, little one?"

"I'm ugly!" the girl sobbed. "Your other granddaughters have long, flowing hair, their teeth are straight, and they have prettier faces than mine. Everyone wants to be their friend because they are beautiful."

Grandmother held her close and said, "So, do you think that being beautiful is what makes a person happy?"

"Yes," wept the little one.

Grandmother looked up towards the sky and said, "Well, we will have to see if that is true."

A single white snowflake fell from the sky, down towards the crying child. It landed on her shoulder and instantly she was transformed into Swan.

Swan was beautiful. Her feathers were brilliant white and her shape was flowing and graceful. But when other birds came to admire her she would hiss at them and chase them away. She stole their food and would not let them live in peace.

Soon she was left alone by all the others. She spent her time drifting by herself on a lonely pond. None of the other birds wanted to be near Swan, even though she was the prettiest of them all. They knew that she was mean and cross inside.

When springtime finally came and the very last snowflake melted, Swan transformed back into the little girl. Grandmother was waiting for her.

Grandmother asked, "So, little one, is it true that beauty is what brings happiness?"

"No, it isn't," her granddaughter replied. "Swan had beautiful feathers, but she was alone and sad."

Grandmother said, "Well, it seems you have learned a valuable lesson."

"Yes," said her granddaughter. "If I want to be happy, I just need to be a beautiful person on the inside."

# Rainbow Trout's Colours

Grandfather and his grandson were working outside, bringing in the winter firewood. The day was dull and rainy, and as they worked the cold water ran down their necks.

The grandson said, "I wish it would never rain. I like the clear sky and the warm sun better."

Grandfather looked at him and said, "Let's take a rest and I'll tell you a story about the rain."

They found a dry spot under Cedar Tree to sit, and Grandfather began. "Down in the lake, Trout once felt the same way you do. He liked summer's sun because food became more plentiful. That is when the water in the lake gets warm and the insects hatch."

"One rainy day, Trout saw Eagle flying overhead and called out to him, 'Eagle, can you fly up into the sky and drag the rain clouds away to the other side of the mountain?'

"Eagle asked, 'So you think it would be good for the rain to go away so you could have sun all the time?'

"'Oh, yes,' said Trout. 'It would be warm and bright and there would be lots of food for me.'

"Eagle thought, 'It looks like I need to teach Trout a lesson.'

"Eagle flew up into the sky and dragged the grey rain clouds to the next valley, letting the bright sun shine down on Trout's lake.

"Trout was very happy. Every day was bright, warm, and cheerful, and there was lots to eat. But after a while things started to change. Trout noticed that the lake's water was not as deep as it used to be. All along the shoreline the lake had receded, leaving nothing but dry mud. Trout also noticed that the insects, who needed those shallows to feed and hatch their eggs, had left. As the water got lower there was less to eat and Trout was finally trapped in a little pond with no food and barely enough room to turn around.

"Trout looked up and saw Eagle watching him from a treetop. Trout called out, 'Eagle, I was wrong. There can be too much sunshine. Now I know that rain is an important part of our world. Without it, the lake and everything I need to live will go away.'

"Eagle flew over the mountain and dragged the clouds back. Just before they covered over the sun, a bright rainbow arched down from the rain clouds and shone on Trout. The colours splashed onto his scales and transformed him into Rainbow Trout."

Grandfather looked up into the sky and said to his grandson, "I accept the cloudy weather, just like Rainbow Trout now does, because I know that without rain there would never be any more rainbows. Remember, everything has a purpose, even though we may not always understand what it is."

# Elk's Antlers

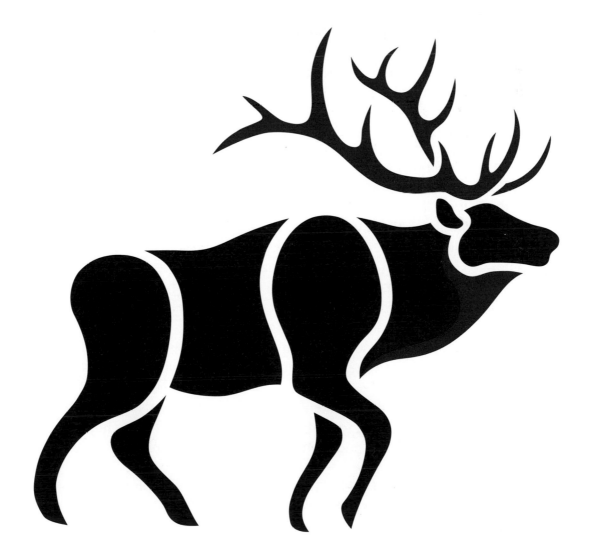

Cedar Tree had grown on the same spot for hundreds of years. His old weathered top had split into a crown of spires, grey from the many storms he had lived through. Still his trunk grew broad and straight and rose to the sky. His roots went deep into the ground and kept him from falling over in even the fiercest winds.

Something was coming to the Valley that put Cedar Tree and all the other trees and creatures of the forest in danger.

Off in town, far away, people were drawing up plans to come into the valley where Cedar Tree lived and cut down the trees. The people were not evil. Most of them just wanted enough wood to build their homes and to keep them warm. But some of the people wanted all the wood to sell and make lots of money.

When Eagle heard of the people's plan, he flew out to the forest and landed on one of Cedar Tree's branches.

Eagle said to Cedar Tree, "People will be coming soon and they plan to cut down all of the forest. They don't know how important trees are to the rest of the forest's animals and birds. All they see is wood for themselves."

Cedar Tree replied, "But we have shared our wood with people before. We gave them bark to weave into cloth and baskets. We have given them the finest spars and masts for their ships. We let them take planks from our sides to build roofs over their homes. They don't need to cut down all the trees. There is lots of wood to share."

Eagle said, "You are very wise, old Cedar Tree. I am going to give you legs so you can go to the people and tell them your stories. Perhaps they will listen to you."

With that, Eagle soared into the sky and transformed Cedar Tree into Elk. Cedar Tree's grey spires became a towering crown of antlers on Elk's head and the trunk emerged as Elk's muscular body, and the deep roots formed into powerful legs.

Elk went to the people and said, "There are many animals, birds, and plants that live in the forest. Each needs the trees for a different reason. Some live in them, some eat their leaves, and others use the wood for their homes. But they all know that they must share the trees."

The people listened to Elk because they could see from his huge antlers that he had lived many years and was very wise.

The people realized that they needed to know more about the ways of nature so they went back with Elk to the forest. There, they learned from the trees, animals, and birds that the forest gives food and homes to many creatures, including people.

Elk said to the people, "Now you understand that if we can learn to live in balance, then the forest can provide for us all."

# Wild Horse

There once was a chestnut-brown stallion named Wild Horse. He was the biggest and bravest of all the horses. He could run faster than the wind and jump over rivers in one leap. Wild Horse was free to do whatever he wanted.

One day Wild Horse came upon Grandfather, who was struggling to haul heavy logs to where he was building a home.

Wild Horse felt sorry for Grandfather and said, "Let me help you."

With the two of them pulling, they easily dragged the big logs through the forest.

Grandfather said, "Thank you, Wild Horse," and gave him a bag of grain as a gift for helping.

Wild Horse helped Grandfather several times over the next few months. He pulled the plough over a new field, and he carried Grandmother to the doctor when she was sick. In exchange, Grandfather shared his grain and hay with Wild Horse.

One day, in mid-winter, the snow was very deep. Grandfather had not seen Wild Horse for a few days, so he went out looking for him. He found Wild Horse trapped in the snow. Wild Horse was hurt, and hungry animals were surrounding him, waiting for him to become too weak to fight them off.

Grandfather chased the wild animals away before they could hurt his friend. Then Grandfather led Wild Horse back to his farm and into the warmth and security of the barn.

Grandfather said to Wild Horse, "You have always offered to help me when I needed it. You are welcome to live in the meadow and spend the nights inside my barn where you will be safe."

Wild Horse replied, "Thank you. It's cold, dark, and dangerous out in the wilderness at night. I would like to live with you and always be close by to help you with your work."

In this way, Man and Wild Horse became partners, each giving something to the other and receiving something of value in return.

# Grey Whale's Wish

Eagle was flying high over the shimmering sea, gliding along on the air currents with his great wings stretched out to each side. Suddenly, a huge creature leapt from the ocean below and fell back with a splash of foam. A few seconds later it jumped again. Eagle was curious, so he flew lower and watched.

It was Grey Whale who was jumping.

Eagle asked him, "Why are you trying to jump up into the sky?"

Grey Whale replied, "I was watching you gliding high above and I thought how wonderful it would be to soar in the sky and see for miles around. I have long fins, just like your wings, so I thought if I could jump high enough I might be able to fly, like you."

Eagle laughed. "It is funny that you wish to fly like me, because I would like to swim like you. I can only catch fish if they come near the surface. If I could swim, then I could chase them, even into the deepest water."

Eagle asked, "If I give you my gift of flight, will you give me your ability to swim? That way we will both have what we really want."

Grey Whale thought that it was a wonderful idea to exchange places, so that is what they did. Grey Whale flew off into the sky and Eagle swam away beneath the waves. At first, Grey Whale liked flying. He could swoop and soar and see for miles around. But after a while he started to get tired. He was so heavy that he had to work very hard to stay up. The hot sun blistered his skin and the wind made his eyes water.

Eagle had a good time chasing all the fish, but soon he was full and could not eat any more. That's when he started to notice that it was very dark and cold under the ocean. His feathers were all soaked and his eyes stung from the salty water. He had to swim all the time because he was so light that every time he stopped he would float back up to the top.

Eventually both of them got too tired. Grey Whale flopped down onto the ocean just as Eagle popped up to the surface.

Grey Whale said to Eagle, "If you don't mind, I would like to go back to the way we were before."

Eagle replied, "Oh, yes, that would make me happy, too."

As Grey Whale swam away, he called to Eagle, "I have learned a lesson from this. From now on, I will be happy with who I am."

# Rockfish Finds a Home

Grandfather sat watching his grandson pack things into a bag. The young man was leaving on another trip, even though he had only returned home a few days earlier.

Grandfather said to him, "Why are you always travelling to new places? Why don't you stay here at home where it is safe and your friends and family are near?"

His grandson replied, "I don't need any place to call home. I like to be free to go wherever I want. Home to me is just wherever I happen to end up each day."

Grandfather looked at him and said, "Let me tell you about Rockfish and his home.

"Rockfish did not always live in that cave in the reef. He used to swim around in the open ocean. He hunted every day for food and spent his nights trying not to become food for someone else.

"His friends asked, 'Why don't you find a safe place like our cave to live in?'

"Rockfish replied, 'I don't need a home. I am free to roam wherever I please while you are stuck in one place all the time.'

"But the waters where Rockfish swam each day are a dangerous place, because that is where Shark lives.

"One day as Rockfish swam near the reef, he came upon Shark, out hunting.

"Shark said to him, 'Well, Rockfish, I think that you shall be my supper tonight.'

"Rockfish looked all around, but all the caves and crevices in the reef already had creatures living in them.

"As Shark came after him he frantically looked for any place to hide.

"A small crack between two rocks came into view. Rockfish squeezed in, just in time to avoid Shark's teeth.

"As Rockfish watched Shark swim away, he said to himself, 'My friends were right. It is important to have a home.'"

Grandfather smiled at his grandson and said, "Rockfish found that constantly moving on was not always good. Sometimes it is wiser to settle down, so you have one safe place to call home."

# Deer's Lesson

It was an early summer morning. The sun glistened off the dew as Deer and her yearling fawn came out of the forest into the meadow.

Deer said to her fawn, "You are growing up. It will soon be time for you to leave my care and start a family of your own."

Her young daughter asked, "Will you teach me how to raise a family before I go?"

Deer replied with a smile, "I have been teaching you that from the day you were born."

Her daughter looked puzzled and said, "I do not remember you ever telling me how to raise a family."

Deer replied, "Oh, but I taught you something new every day. Remember when I showed you how to find the tender shoots hidden under the winter grass? Or when you were cold during the snow and I cuddled up to you to keep you warm? Or the time I showed you how to hide from Cougar by staying so still?"

"Yes, I remember those times. But how does that help me raise my family?"

Deer answered, "When you are faced with similar circumstances you will remember the lessons I showed you, and you will know what to do."

"Is that how you learned to be a good parent?" her daughter asked.

"Yes," Deer replied. "That is the way all parents teach their youngsters. The examples we set every day are the examples our young will in turn pass on to the next generation."

The next year Deer watched her daughter take her own newborn fawn and show him how to find the tender grass. Deer saw that when the cold wind blew, her daughter would block it with her body to protect her son. And when danger was near, the fawn would hide motionless in the grass just as his mother had taught him to.

Deer said to her daughter, "You see, every day your son is learning how to be a good parent, just as you learned from me."

# Rabbit's Great Escape

The little girl came to Grandmother and sat down beside her on the porch swing. They rocked back and forth and watched the sun set in the western sky. Her little granddaughter seemed sad, so Grandmother asked, "How come you haven't got your smile with you today?"

Her granddaughter replied, "I'm sad because the bigger kids are always taking my things and being mean to me. Some day I hope I will grow up to be a giant, and then if I want something I'll just take it."

Grandmother held her hand and said, "Little one, it is not always best to be biggest. The story of Rabbit will help you understand what I mean.

"Rabbit lived in the meadow on the edge of the forest. She and her family spent their days timidly hopping through the tall grass and flowers in search of sweet clover and other things to eat. Rabbit liked to live in peace.

"One day, Cougar came to the meadow looking for food. Cougar said to Rabbit, 'Well, you would certainly be a good dinner for me.'

"Rabbit replied, 'Yes, I probably would if you could catch me. But I don't think you can.'

"Cougar laughed, 'Are you joking? I am 100 times your size. My legs are longer than yours and my muscles are stronger. You'd better start running, because here I come.'

"Rabbit said, 'All right, but you won't be having me for dinner tonight.' And off she ran.

"Cougar leapt after her and the chase was on. Every time Cougar was about to catch her, Rabbit made a quick zigzag to escape. Rabbit ran across an opening in the meadow and Cougar made a dash for her. Rabbit shot into a thicket of blackberry vines. Cougar crashed in close behind.

"Rabbit knew about a pathway under the sharp thorns. But Cougar was too big. He ended up getting pricked and scratched all over.

"Big Cougar ran crying back into the forest while clever little Rabbit smiled and went back to eating her clover."

Grandmother hugged her little granddaughter and said, "You see, in life it is not the biggest or fastest that wins. By being clever, you come out ahead in the end."

# Fox's Flame

Grandfather gently placed some dry shavings of wood on a tiny ember and blew until a thin wisp of smoke came up. When the shavings caught fire, he carefully added more wood until the campfire's flames licked up towards the night sky and sent glowing sparks sailing into the darkness. The fire crackled as if beckoning the family closer.

Grandfather gathered his grandchildren around him and together they stared at the bright orange flames.

"Who saw Fox today when we were up walking in the alpine meadow?" he asked.

The littlest of the grandchildren, nestled under his arm, answered, "I did, Grandfather."

"Well, you certainly have good eyes. It is very special to see Fox these days," said Grandfather. "When I was young like you, I used to see Fox all the time.

"One day Fox said to me, 'Why don't people like me?'

"I said, 'What makes you think we don't like you?'

"'Well,' said Fox, 'the other day a farmer chased me from his field where I was hunting for mice. Once a trapper caught me in a steel trap and by the time I was able to escape my leg was damaged forever. Then another time I ate some poisoned food that a man had left near my home and I got very sick. That is why I think people don't like me.'

"'I don't blame you,' I said. 'We have not been very nice to you. After all, you were here long before we came.'

"'Back then there were many more of us.' said Fox. 'Every field had a family living in it. But now the few of us that are left have to hide in the bushes and creep about at night to avoid being hurt by people.'"

Grandfather put another stick on the fire and continued the story. "I realized that Fox was like a fire that we had forgotten. Fox's life used to be a roaring flame and now it was only a glowing ember. My friends and I decided to help.

"We said to Fox, 'Help us teach other people about you. When they understand, they will want to save you too.'

"So that is what we did. We protected Fox, gave him a place to live, and shared with him. Slowly and surely his flame of life became stronger and his family started to grow.

"Fox said to us, 'Thank you. I am glad that you cared enough to give up some of what you had in order to give me and my family enough room to live. I hope someday all people will learn to share like you have, so that no creature will have its flame die forever.'

"Today, when we see Fox, he is the colour of fire with a tail shaped like a flame licking into the sky. Seeing him reminds us that any creature's flame, including ours, can go out if we don't share our world."

# Raven and the Two-Headed Salmon

Grandfather was in the mood to tell a story. He sat with his two granddaughters on his knees and said, "Let me tell you about how your two fathers and I once caught the biggest salmon in the world.

"Many years ago the three of us decided to go fishing, so we headed out in our boat to that narrow channel between those two islands over there.

"Raven, who was flying overhead, saw us and said to himself, 'I think I will play a little joke on these fishermen.'

"Raven watched your fathers let down their fishing lines on either side of the boat. Then he plunged into the ocean behind our boat and transformed himself into a giant two-headed salmon. He swam up to where the two baits trailed in the water, and with each of his two heads he grabbed onto a hook.

"Back in the boat I saw both poles pulling and yelled, 'Pull in your lines! You both have a fish on.'

"Your fathers each grabbed their poles and started to reel in their fish.

"But I noticed that whenever one salmon would run, the other would run too. And when one salmon would shake, so would the other. It didn't take long to realize they had the same fish on both lines.

"One of your fathers said to the other, 'Your line must be snagged on mine. You must cut your line so I can bring in my salmon.'

"The other replied, 'Maybe your line is snagged on mine and it's you that should cut your line.'

"The argument continued as they both tried to reel in the enormous fish.

"That is when my friend Kingfisher was attracted by all the shouting and flew over.

"Kingfisher said to me, 'I think this is the work of our mischievous friend, Raven. I'll try to help you out.'

"Kingfisher dove under the water and started pecking at the tail of Raven's two-headed salmon. Raven tried to outrun Kingfisher, but as he darted past our boat I dipped in my big net and pulled him in.

"Your fathers were amazed that their lines had not been snagged. Instead they saw that a giant two-headed salmon had bitten both their hooks.

"One of them said, 'It is so big. Lucky we had two lines hooked to it because I do not think I could have brought it in by myself.'

"The other said, 'Without your help it would have pulled me out of the boat and into the ocean.'

"I said, 'I think you both have Kingfisher to thank. Without him, neither of you would have a fish.'

"Raven waited until we weren't looking, and then he transformed himself back into his bird form. He flew away, leaving behind our gigantic fish. It was so big that it took all three of us just to carry it from the boat. People came from miles around to see our enormous two-headed salmon."

One of his granddaughters smiled and said, "Grandfather, I think part of Raven's mischief must have been left behind in that fish, because every time you tell this story, that salmon gets bigger and bigger."

# About the Author

Born in Vancouver, British Columbia, in 1953, Robert James (Jim) Challenger lives in Victoria, on the southern end of Vancouver Island.

Jim has spent his life absorbing all the stories the Northwest Coast has to offer. A keen observer of the natural behaviour of wildlife, he has developed his own style of artwork that captures the essence of the many creatures that live around him.

Jim is an accomplished artist and stone carver, and has sold his beach-stone and glass carvings to collectors around the world. His highly sought-after form-line designs capture the shape and movement of his subjects while maintaining the simplicity of flowing lines and shapes.

Jim's stories and designs bring a unique perspective to how we can learn from nature's examples in the world that surrounds us. For more information about the author, you can visit his website: www.rjchallenger.com